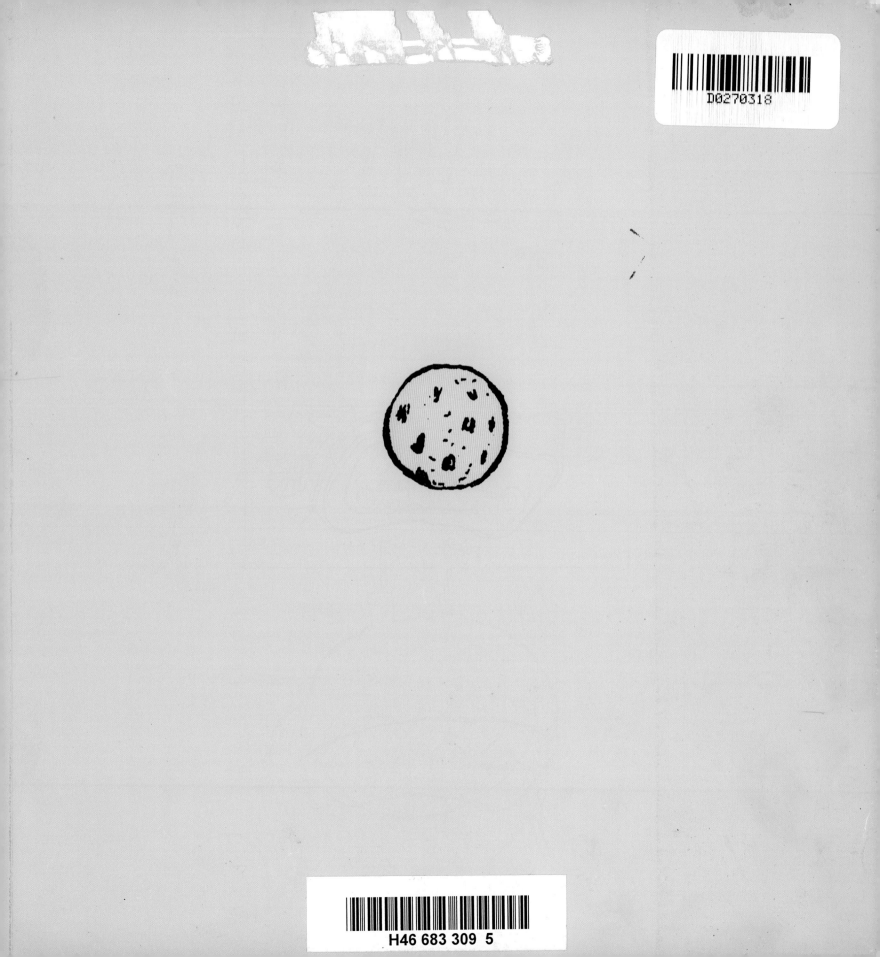

Raintree is an imprint of Capstone Global Library Limited,
a company incorporated in England and Wales having its
registered office at 7 Pilgrim Street, London, EC4V 6LB –
Registered company number: 6695582

To contact Raintree:
Phone: 0845 6044371
Fax: + 44 (0) 1865 312263
Email: myorders@raintreepublishers.co.uk
Outside the UK please telephone +44 1865 312262.

First published by © Picture Window Books in 2011
First published in the United Kingdom in paperback in 2014
The moral rights of the proprietor have been asserted.

Designer: Kay Fraser
Editor: Catherine Veitch
Originated by Capstone Global Library Ltd
Printed and bound in China

ISBN 978 1 4062 6620 7 (paperback)
18 17 16 15 14 13
10 9 8 7 6 5 4 3 2 1

British Library Cataloguing in Publication Data
A full catalogue record for this book is available from
the British Library.

STROPPY STAN

written by Adam and Charlotte Guillain
illustrated by Sarah Horne

Stan was famous for being **stroppy**.

He got stroppy when he was told off for playing ball games in the house.

When his sister's biscuit had more
chocolate chips in it than his,
Stan got **very** stroppy.

And when Stan lost a board game...

Woah! Stand back!

"This isn't the dinosaur backpack I wanted!" Stan **shouted** at his mum.

"I hope you don't **scream** and **shout** and throw your arms about like that at school," his mum told him. "Stop being **stroppy!**"

But at school Stan wasn't stroppy.

He couldn't **scream** and **shout** and throw his arms and legs about because his teacher had a special saying.

When things do not go your way, stay calm. Don't scream and shout. Try a little give and take and things might just work out.

So when Stan was given crayons instead of
pens he tried **very** hard to stay calm.

And when he found himself at the back of the
dinner queue he didn't **scream** or **shout**,
even though he **really** wanted to.

And even when he got a pretty **pink** napkin with his lunch, Stan didn't get stroppy.

"Give and take has got nothing to do with *it*," Stan grumbled. "That saying is just **stupid!**"

Well, at least his family didn't say such things.

After school Stan wanted to watch his **favourite** film.

"But I want to watch *A Pony Called Trouble!*"
his little sister protested. She started to
scream and **shout**.

Stan was about to lose his temper and
scream and **shout** right back
but then ...

"When things do not go your way, stay calm. Don't **scream** and **shout**," Stan told his sister, calmly. "Try a little **give** and **take** and things might just work out."

"What did he say?" everyone **gasped**.

Stan felt rather **proud** of himself.

"When things do not go your way, stay calm. Don't **scream** and **shout**," he repeated. "Try a little give and take and things might just work out."

For a moment no one spoke. **Then** -

"Does that mean Stan shouldn't **shout** at me for having more chocolate chips than him?" his little sister asked.

"And when you lose a board game perhaps you shouldn't get **stroppy**?" Stan's dad asked him.

"And if the dinosaur backpacks are all sold out perhaps Stan shouldn't **stamp** on the one I bought him instead?" Mum added.

Stan **gulped.** He was starting to feel
a bit less stroppy...

"But that's just a **silly** saying my teacher made up to make us be nice to each other at school," Stan pleaded. "I can **scream** and **shout** as much as I like at home."

"I think that silly saying sounds like **great** advice for home, too," said Dad. "**I agree**," said Mum.

"Does that mean we have to watch my film **and** Stan's film?" asked Stan's little sister.

Stan wanted to **scream**.

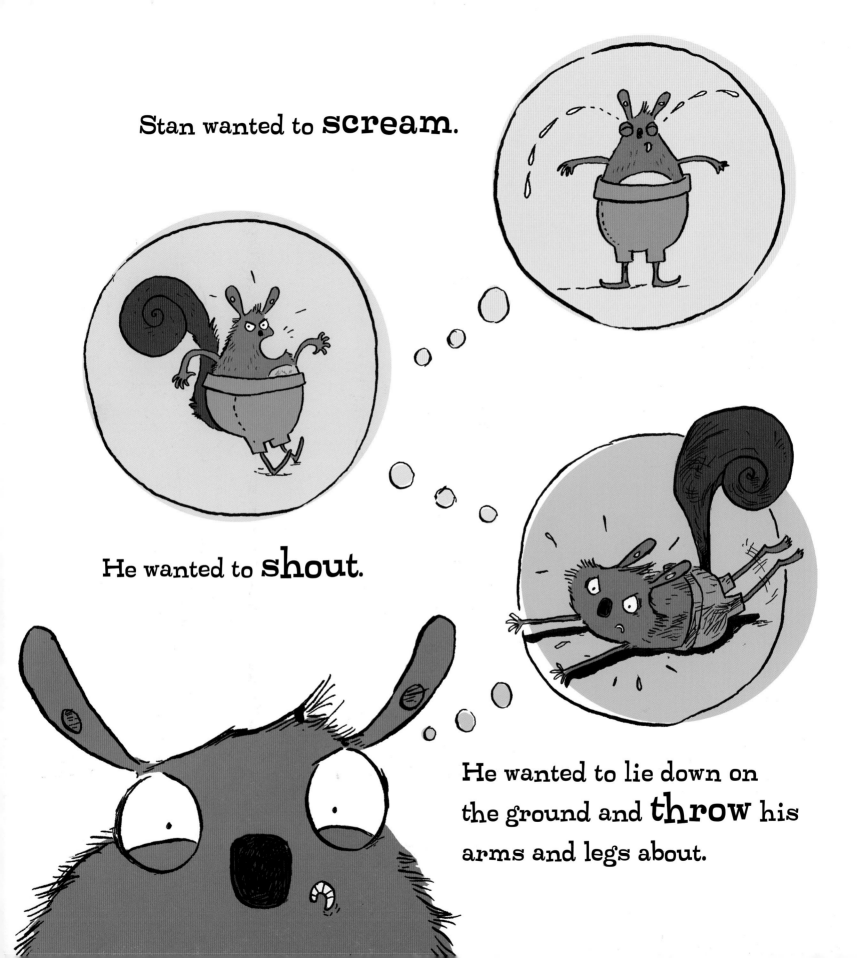

He wanted to **shout**.

He wanted to lie down on the ground and **throw** his arms and legs about.

But he didn't.

And everything **worked out**. Just as his teacher had said.

A PONY CALLED TROUBLE